45 p

The Young World Library is a series designed for the
young reader. The stories are taken from some of the
world's best-known novels, plays, legends, operas and
ballets. They have been simplified and re-told in a way
which keeps close to the spirit of the original, while bringing
everything within the immediate grasp of the young
reader's understanding of words. Equally important are
the illustrations, which have been chosen both to delight
the eye and to match the special character of each story.
Thus the Young World Library offers young readers a
unique stepping stone towards the use and enjoyment of
books. It also introduces them in a lively, up-to-date way
to many famous stories and characters from the
wonderful world of literature and the performing arts.

Series Editor: Alan Blackwood

Cover design by Hildegarde Bone

© 1973 Thomas Nelson & Sons Limited
S.B.N. 72380961 5
Printed in Great Britain by A. Wheaton & Co., Exeter

THE GREAT WHITE WHALE

Adapted and told by
Edward Holmes

Illustrated by
Charles Front

Based on the novel *Moby Dick* by
Herman Melville

NELSON
YOUNG WORLD

Moby Dick was the biggest whale that ever was. And he was white, like a huge ghost swimming through the darkness of the oceans. Nobody knew how old he was, and simple sailors used to say that he had lived forever. They said that he was wicked, too. For sure, he was very cunning.

Moby Dick was a sperm whale,
and sperm whales were hunted
by men in whalers—sailing
ships which often were smaller
than the whales they hunted.
The oil from these huge whales
was used in the lamps of those
days. One ship that hunted
whales for their oil was
called the "Pequod".

The captain of the "Pequod" was Captain Ahab, a grim and fearsome old man who paced his quarter-deck on one real leg and one false one—a shining white leg made out of whale ivory. The real leg whose place it took had been bitten off—by Moby Dick. Captain Ahab hated the great white whale with a deadly hatred, and lived for just one thing, revenge on the monster who had taken away his leg. His crew were a tough and desperate bunch—even among whale-men, who risked their lives daily in the pursuit of their monstrous quarry. One day, he called them all together on his after-deck.

As they watched he nailed a
golden coin, a doubloon, to
the mast. " 'tis a sixteen
dollar gold piece, men," he
cried. "D'you see it?"

"Whosoever of ye finds me a
white whale with a wrinkled
brow and a crooked jaw, and
three holes in his starboard
fluke, shall have this gold
ounce, my boys!" The seamen
cheered, and Tashtego, a red
indian, one of the ship's
three heathen harpooners,
cried out, "Captain Ahab,
that white whale must be the
same that some call Moby Dick!"

"Moby Dick!" shouted Ahab "Do
you know him then, Tash?"
"Does he fan-tail a little odd
as he dives, then?" asked the
indian, and Daggoo, a huge
negro harpooner, cried, "And
does he spout very bushy, and
mighty quick, Captain Ahab?"
And Queequeg, the cannibal
islander, shouted "And has he
many harpoons, all twisted,
in him too?"

"Aye, Queequeg!" thundered
Ahab, "the harpoons lie all
twisted in him; aye, Daggoo
his spout is big, like a shock
of wheat; aye, Tashtego, he
fan-tails like a split jib in
a squall when he dives. Death
and devils, men, it is Moby
Dick you have seen, Moby Dick!"
Then up spoke Starbuck, the
Quaker first mate; "Captain
Ahab, was it not Moby Dick
that took off thy leg?"
"Who told thee that?" cried
Ahab, "aye, Starbuck, it was
Moby Dick that dismasted me,
and made a poor pegging lubber
of me for ever and a day!
It was Moby Dick that brought
me to this dead stump that I
stand on now!" Ahab shook his
fists at the sky, and shouted.

"Aye! I'll chase him to
perdition's flames before I
give him up. This is what you
have shipped for, men; to chase
the white whale over all the
earth, till he spouts black
blood, and rolls fin out!"

So it was, the beginning of
the final hunt for the white
monster of Ahab's nightmares.
On and on they sailed, until
it seemed that Ahab was another
Flying Dutchman, doomed to
voyage on forever. Whales they
sighted, but never Moby Dick.
Ships they met; ship's masters
they questioned.

"Have ye seen a white whale?"
Time and again, the answer
was "No!" Then some they met
had seen Moby Dick—seen
him in the tropics, seen him
in the arctic seas of the far
north, seen him down in the
Pacific, low down where the ice
begins . . . Time and distance
were nothing to Moby Dick.

And at last the chase was
closing. Moby Dick had been
seen short days ago . . . And
Ahab's vast knowledge of
whales and their ways told
him they were getting near.

Then, at last, came the night
when Ahab stepped out of his
cabin, and sniffed the air
like an old hunting dog.
A whale was near! Soon all
on board could catch the scent
of a sperm-whale on the night
air. Ahab corrected course
a little, to follow the scent,
and shortened sail for speed.
At dawning, there was the
smooth wake of a great whale . . .

Ahab himself climbed the main
mast to join the look-outs,
and it was his voice which
cried out; "There she blows!
A hump like a snow-hill!
It is Moby Dick!"

"I keep the doubloon!" cried
Ahab. "I only could have seen
the white whale first! There
she blows! There again—and
again! He's going to sound!
In stunsails! Down top-gallant!
Man the boats! There go the
flukes! Moby Dick is going
to dive! Lower me to my
boat, Mr Starbuck!"

Soon all the boats were
away—small rowing boats—
while Starbuck stayed in
charge of "Pequod". Ahab
led the hunt in his boat.
Moby Dick rested in the sea.
Then, suddenly, he arched
his whole huge body into
the air, dived, and was
gone into the depths.

The boats floated stilly,
waiting for Moby Dick to
re-appear. Suddenly,
Tashtego shouted: "The
birds—look—the birds!"
The sea birds, which had been
flying over the white whale
were now flying in a line
towards Ahab's boat. Ahab
stared down into the water.

Far down below, Ahab made
out a white shape, rushing
upwards to the surface!
This was what the sea birds
had seen! Ahab gave one
great sweep with the steering
oar, and whirled the boat
aside from the uprushing Moby
Dick. Then he leaped into
the bows, and seized a harpoon.
Now, thanks to Ahab's prompt
action, the boat was facing
the whale's attack. Instantly
the monster shifted his course,
turned half on his back, and
came up under Ahab's boat
with open mouth in the manner
of a shark. The tremendous
jaws closed across the bows
of the row-boat, and lifted
it into the air. Moby Dick
shook the boat savagely.

The crew tumbled into the
water. Only Ahab remained,
tearing with his bare hands
at the jaws of the monster.
Then he, too, fell into
the sea.

Moby Dick drew off a little,
and swam round the wreckage
he had wrought, his wicked
eye on Ahab's grey head.
Starbuck brought the "Pequod"
to the rescue, bringing it
between Moby Dick and his
victims. Then the other
row-boats could move in,
and rescue the men in
the water. They dragged
Ahab out, half dead.

At first it seemed that even
Ahab's iron frame had cracked
in the ordeal, for he lay
like a corpse in the boat's
bottom. But he lived to
fight another day—and
so did Moby Dick. Next day
they sighted him again,
leaping like a gigantic
salmon out of the water.

Again leaving Starbuck in
charge of the "Pequod",
Ahab again led three boats
into battle. This time
Moby Dick turned to the
attack, and churning the sea
into white foam with the fury
of his charge, rushed in
among them. Three harpoons
drove into his body, but he
heeded them not, nor the
stout lines they carried.
Back he turned, throwing the
lines into a hopeless tangle.
The three boats were being
dragged helplessly hither
and yon by the charging
monster, thrown about like
toys in the fury of white
foam thrown up by Moby Dick's
threshing tail. Back he
turned again . . .

The harpoons held fast in
Moby Dick's body, anchoring
the three boats to him. Only
Ahab remained cool, and cut
his harpoon line with a slash
of the ship's knife.

The other two boats, still
tied to Moby Dick smashed
together, and shattered. Then
Moby Dick vanished beneath
the sea in the midst of the
tangle of men and wreckage
that he had made.

For a moment there was a
pause, then he thundered up
from beneath Ahab's boat,
and smashed it into the air
like a matchbox.

The boat tumbled, upside down,
while Ahab and his men fell
helpless into the sea.
Moby Dick swam away, trailing
broken harpoon lines behind
him, while Starbuck in the
"Pequod" picked the seamen
out of the water. Then,
under full sail, and driven
by the awful wrath of Ahab,
they pursued Moby Dick until
night fell. Any other captain
would have given up the chase,
but not Ahab. The cost of
hunting Moby Dick was mounting
high, but with every battle
that the monster white whale
won, Captain Ahab's fury
against him mounted tenfold.
His hatred for the whale was
a madness which gripped him,
from which he would never escape.

Night fell, but night brought
no rest for the crew of the
"Pequod". First, there were
the smashed boats to make
good, and the ship's carpenter
hammered and sawed and
laboured to complete the
work, and directed the
unskilled work of the crewmen
who helped him.

Harpoons were needed, the
iron-barbed wooden lances
by which the whalers
anchored their lines into
the tough flesh of the
monsters they hunted. All
night long the smith's
furnace glowed, and his
hammer rang, as he forged
new harpoons for the morrow.

At dawn on the morrow there
was no sign of Moby Dick, and
all they could do was follow
a course that Ahab, in some
strange way, guessed to be the
right one. It was gone noon
before they sighted the vast
spout of him in the distance.

G.W.W.—C

Ahab watched him for a while
from the high mast-head.
Then he was lowered to lead
the three small boats once
more into the battle with the
great white whale. They
pulled away towards him, and
were out of the sighting of
him when he sounded, low as
they were in the water. But
they saw the signal from the
"Pequod's" mast heads, that
told that he had dived, and
where. Ahab held the boats
on their course, intending
to be near at hand when Moby
Dick rose once more from
the deeps. Then they floated,
waiting on the ocean, all the
men bewitched into silence by
the knowledge that the final
battle was at hand.

Then with a thunder of sound,
Moby Dick shot from the sea,
bedraggled with harpoons and
lances, trailing broken lines.
A great cascade of water
filled the air as he fell back
into the sea, thrashing and
smashing with his vast tail.

Head on, he came churning among them, his vast bulk looming above them like a cliff. Once more he flailed boats and men into useless wreckage in the sea. But, strangely, Moby Dick left Ahab's boat almost without a scar.

Strangely again, Moby Dick
turned away from Ahab—
swam off—but then turned,
and hurled himself like a
giant battering ram at
the "Pequod".

The force of the impact rent
the ship apart; shattered
timbers let the sea in.
Then the whale went under the
"Pequod", surfaced on the other
side—and Ahab and Moby Dick
were face to face. Ahab drove
his harpoon deep into the
monster's flesh.

It was a death blow. The
stricken whale flew forward;
the harpoon line fled out from
the line tub, almost igniting
the wood with its speed. It
ran foul, and Ahab stooped
to clear it; he did clear it,
but a flying turn caught him . . .

A flying turn of harpoon line
caught Ahab around the neck,
and voicelessly he was shot
out of the boat, before the
crew knew that he was gone.
Next instant, the heavy eye-
splice in the rope's final
end shot into the sea.

For an instant the bewitched
ship's crew stood still, stunned
by events. Then they turned,
turned towards their only
hope of salvation. "The ship!
Great God, where is the ship?"

It was a terrible sight that
met the eyes of Ahab's stricken
crewmen. Through the turmoil
of thrown-up spray, they saw
her sliding like a ghost
into the depths of the
ocean, her hull shattered and
leaking in a hundred places
from the monstrous hammer-
blow of Moby Dick's vast
head. Now only the "Pequod's"
masts were out of the
water, and there, still in
their once lofty perches,
the look-outs still kept
their vigil, frozen there by
terror, by fate, or perhaps
by faithfulness. Now they too
were going under, until only
the topmost tip of the main-
mast, where Tashtego perched,
remained above water.

Tashtego had been in the
act of nailing a pennant
to the mast-head, and thus
he went to his doom, the hammer
raised as he struck final
useless blows.

43

So vanished the "Pequod",
plunging to the depths in the
wake of Moby Dick and old Ahab.
And the vast whirlpool of
her sinking sucked down the
last remaining boat, and every
last fragment of shattered
wreckage, and frail humanity.

For the ghastly hatred between
two creatures, Captain Ahab
and Moby Dick, the final price
had been paid. The whirlpool
of "Pequod's" sinking smoothed
out, and the waves rolled on
as they had done since the
beginning of time . . .